E
WEB

1/14

MONSTER HEROES

THE GHOST TRAP

BY BLAKE HOENA
ILLUSTRATED BY DAVE BARDIN

STONE ARCH BOOKS
a capstone-imprint

Monster Heroes is published by
Stone Arch Books, a Capstone Imprint
1710 Roe Crest Drive
North Mankato, Minnesota 56003
www.mycapstone.com

Library of Congress Cataloging-in-Publication Data
Names: Hoena, B. A., author. | Bardin, Dave (Illustrator), illustrator
Title: The ghost trap / by Blake Hoena ; illustrated by Dave Bardin. Description:
North Mankato, Minnesota : Stone Arch Books, a Capstone imprint,   [2017]
Series: Monster heroes | Summary: Will is a quiet and gentle ghost,
so when three bully ghosts set out to scare the people at Hill House,
he and his other monster friends come up with a plan to stop them.
Identifiers: LCCN 2016006105 | ISBN 9781496537577 (library binding)
Subjects: LCSH: Ghost stories. | Monsters—Juvenile fiction. |
Friendship—Juvenile fiction. | Heroes—Juvenile fiction. |
Bullies—Juvenile fiction. | CYAC: Ghosts—Fiction. |Monsters—Fiction.
|Friendship—Fiction. | Heroes—Fiction. | Bullying—Fiction.
Classification: LCC PZ7.H67127 Gh 2017 | DDC 813.6—dc23
LC record available at http://lccn.loc.gov/2016006105

Book design by: Ted Williams
Photo credit: Krithika Mahalingam Photography (mahalphoto.com), pg 94,
Shutterstock, kasha_malasha, design element

Printed and bound in the United States of America.
009666F16

TABLE OF CONTENTS

MINA (the Vampire)

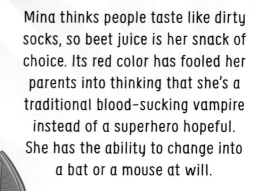

Mina thinks people taste like dirty socks, so beet juice is her snack of choice. Its red color has fooled her parents into thinking that she's a traditional blood-sucking vampire instead of a superhero hopeful. She has the ability to change into a bat or a mouse at will.

Brian is the brainy one among his friends. Unlike other zombies, Brian prefers tofu to brains. No matter what sort of trouble is brewing, Brian always comes up with a plan to save the day, like a true superhero.

BRIAN (the Zombie)

WILL

Will is quite shy. Luckily he can turn invisible any time he wants because he is a ghost. When Will is doing good deeds, he likes to remain unseen. His invisibility helps him act brave like a real superhero.

With a wave of her wand and a poetic chant, Linda can reverse any magical curse. She hopes to use her magic to help people, just like a superhero would.

LINDA (the Witch)

BULLY GHOSTS

Will hurried through the halls of Frankenstein Elementary. He was on his way to his computer class. As always, he was running late.

He zipped around a werewolf. He zoomed through an ogre. Then he floated over a mummy.

In the classroom, Will saw Jim, Scott, and Kip. They were scary ghosts. Even though Will was a ghost, he didn't like to scare people.

Will and his friends weren't like other monsters. They didn't scare people or haunt houses. His friends wanted to be superheroes and save the day.

Will sat down in front of the other ghosts. As he waited for his computer to turn on, he listened to them.

"A new family moved into the old Hill House," Jim said.

"That's the place by the cemetery, right?" Scott asked.

"Yeah, across from Shirley Jackson's tomb," Kip added.

Just then, Will's computer beeped. The other ghosts stopped talking. Will looked back. They were staring at him.

"Should we ask Will to join us?" Jim asked.

Scott shook his head no. "He's a scaredy cat."

"Yeah! He couldn't even scare a cat, either," Kip added.

The three ghosts moaned loudly. That's what ghosts did when they thought something was funny.

"Wh-wh-where are you going?" Will asked.

"To the Hill House," Scott said.

"Yeah, to haunt some people," Jim added.

"Want to come?" Kip asked.

"N-n-no," Will whispered. He turned back to his computer.

"That's what I thought," Scott said.

Will couldn't let the mean ghosts haunt people. He rushed to meet his friends at lunch. He knew they could help him.

CHAPTER

SUPER MONSTER FRIENDS

At lunch, Will sat with his friends. Brian munched on a tofu brainwich. Mina slurped some beet juice. And Linda ate something too disgusting and smelly to describe.

Will told them about Jim, Scott, and Kip.

"They want to scare the people who moved into the old Hill House," Will said. "And they are going to do it soon."

"We can't let them do that," Linda said.

"We just need a plan," Brian said.

The friends thought and ate. Then they ate some more and thought some more.

"What are ghosts afraid of?" Brian asked.

"People laughter," Will said.

"What?" Linda said in surprise.

"No way!" Mina shouted.

"Like chuckles and giggles?" Brian asked.

Will nodded. He said, "Ghosts like to scare people to hear them shout and scream. But when people laugh, they sound creepy. Ghosts think that's scary."

"That's so weird! But it does give me an idea," Brian said.

The friends leaned in as Brian told them his plan. As always, Brian came up with the perfect idea.

That afternoon, the friends met at their secret hideout. It was a tree house high up in the branches of a big old oak tree. The tree grew in the middle of the cemetery.

"Are you sure the plan will work?" Will asked.

He was nervous. He didn't want to make the mean ghosts mad. Brian lumbered over to Will. He put an arm around the ghost.

"Don't worry," Brian said. "It will definitely make people laugh."

SOCKS AND UNDERPANTS

The friends headed over to the old Hill House and hid. A few minutes later, they saw Jim, Scott, and Kip.

"Are you ready, Will?" Brian whispered.

Will nodded and then floated over to the mean ghosts.

"Can I join you?" Will asked.

"The more the scarier," Scott moaned.

The ghosts floated through one of the walls in the house. Once they were out of sight, Will's friends went into action.

Poof! Mina changed into a bat. She flew through a window into the laundry room. Brian lumbered over to the door. He got ready to push the doorbell.

Linda waved her wand. She chanted, "Creakity creak, stay sound asleep until you hear the ding-a-ling of the doorbell ring!" Then she cast her spell. *Bam*!

Inside the house, the people fell asleep and snored loudly.

"Ahhhooooooo," Jim groaned.

"Booga-booga-booga!" Scott shouted.

"Eeeeeeeeeee," Kip screeched.

No one in the house stirred. All the ghosts could hear were people snoring in the rooms above.

Will floated over to where Mina was hiding in the laundry room. He grabbed a basket of dirty socks and underpants that Mina had found.

"Try putting these on," Will said to the mean ghosts. "It will be really scary."

Just then the doorbell rang, and the people woke up. At the top of the stairs stood a boy and a girl. Jim, Scott, and Kip turned to scare the kids.

But ghosts are invisible. All the kids saw were socks and underpants floating in the air.

The kids giggled and chuckled and snorted with laughter.

"Oh, no!" Jim shouted. "Not laughing!"

"Ahhhh!" Scott screamed. "People Laughter is so scary!"

"Let's get out of here!" Kip yelled.

The ghosts dashed through a wall and disappeared into the night. Will joined his friends at the front door.

"Just like superheroes, we saved the day!" Linda said.

"We sure did! Now let's get out of here," Brian said. "This place is seriously creepy!"

DAVE BARDIN

Dave Bardin studied illustration at Cal State Fullerton while working as an art teacher. As an artist, Dave has worked on many different projects for television, books, comics, and animation. In his spare time Dave enjoys watching documentaries, listening to podcasts, traveling, and spending time with friends and family. He works out of Los Angles, CA.

BLAKE A. HOENA

Blake A. Hoena grew up in central Wisconsin, where he wrote stories about robots conquering the moon and trolls lumbering around the woods behind his parents' house. He now lives in Minnesota and continues to write about fun things like space aliens and superheroes. Blake has written more than fifty chapter books and graphic novels for children.

GHOST'S GLOSSARY

brainwich—a sandwich popular with zombies

cauldron—a black pot, often used by witches to make potions

haunt—to visit, as in a ghostly visit

lumbered—moved in a slow, awkward way; the only way zombies move

mummy—a dead, preserved body; also a monster that looks like it is wrapped up in bandages

ogre—a large giant known for eating people

tofu—food made from soybeans, often used as a meat substitute

tomb—a large, underground vault where the dead are buried

werewolf—a person who turns into a wolf-like monster during a full moon

THINK ABOUT IT

1. In this story, each of the characters plays a part in the plan to stop the mean ghosts. What might have happened if one of the characters couldn't do their part?

2. Shirley Jackson is the author of the very scary novel *The Haunting of Hill House.* To purposefully mention someone or something in a story is an allusion. Why do you think the author used the allusion of Shirley Jackson's name?

3. At the beginning of the story, Will is scared of the other ghosts. How do you think he felt at the end? Why?

WRITE ABOUT IT

1. Write a paragraph describing how Will felt when the other ghosts were making fun of him in the computer lab.

2. The ghosts in this story are scared of laughter. Write a paragraph about something you are scared of.

3. Pick one of the mean ghosts and write a story from his point of view. How did he feel after they left the house? Did he ever haunt people again?